HOCKEY TIMEOUT

Irene Punt

illustrations by
Gary O'Brien

Scholastic Canada Ltd.
Toronto New York London Auckland Sydney
Mexico City New Delhi Hong Kong Buenos Aires

Scholastic Canada Ltd.
604 King Street West, Toronto, Ontario M5V 1E1, Canada

Scholastic Inc.
557 Broadway, New York, NY 10012, USA

Scholastic Australia Pty Limited
PO Box 579, Gosford, NSW 2250, Australia

Scholastic New Zealand Limited
Private Bag 94407, Botany, Manukau 2163, New Zealand

Scholastic Children's Books
Euston House, 24 Eversholt Street, London NW1 1DB, UK

www.scholastic.ca

Library and Archives Canada Cataloguing in Publication
Punt, Irene, 1955-, author
Hockey timeout / Irene Punt ; illustrated by Gary O'Brien.

ISBN 978-1-4431-4649-4 (softcover)

I. O'Brien, Gary (Gary John), illustrator II. Title.

PS8581.U56H64 2018   jC813'.54   C2018-901942-5

6 5 4 3 2 1   Printed in Canada 121   18 19 20 21 22

MIX
Paper from
responsible sources
FSC® C004071

Contents

*To my mom, my boys and
my friends — Wendy, Denise,
Laura, Joanne, Anne, Michele, Julie,
Pam and Carol's mother-in-law —
who have given me high-fives
when I needed them. With love and
appreciation.*

— I. P.

Cleanup

WHEEE! WHEEE!

Coach Howie blew his whistle at the end of Saturday hockey practice.

"Good job, Hawks! Now let's go!" He waved his hand in a big circle above his head. That was Coach Howie's signal to collect the pucks and get off the ice.

"Okay," sighed Tom. He was not ready to quit, even though his legs burned and his equipment was soaking wet from sweat. He loved hockey practices. He had never missed one.

"I'll get the puck bucket," Tom called. Coach Howie gave him a thumbs-up.

Tom skated over to the players' box and grabbed the empty bucket. He put it down at centre ice and looked around for Jordan, Mark, Stuart and Harty, his best friends. He loved playing with them on the Glenlake Hawks because they made hockey fun.

Jordan, their goalie, scooped pucks out of the net with his big goalie stick and shot them down the ice for Tom to put into the bucket.

Grrrrr. Jordan's stomach growled for lunch.

PLUNK! PLUNK! PLUNK! Mark plopped three pucks into the bucket.

"Now that's a bucket trick! Get it? Three goals is a hat trick!" Mark laughed. He liked to be funny.

Harty and Stuart were kicking the pucks

over to Tom. They looked like soccer players until Stuart accidentally stepped on a runaway puck. *SWOOOOOSH!* He slid and fell, knocking the bucket over.

"Oops! Sorry!"

Everyone was helping with cleanup . . . except Sam. He was at the far end of the rink practising his shots.

Sam skated back and forth across the ice. He stickhandled the puck perfectly. He took a shot. The puck soared into the middle of the empty net.

"GOAL!" Sam raised his arms. He kicked one leg and cheered in celebration: "Yahoo!"

"He shoots. He scores!" cheered Mark. "Wow! Sam's getting good!"

"I'm glad Sam's on *our* team!" said Stuart, grinning. "He's our big time goal getter!"

The giant gates at the back of the arena were pushed open by the rink keeper. Eager players waiting for the next ice time watched by the glass.

The Zamboni started up and cranked into gear. *GRZZZ-GERR.*

It pulled out from its parking stall and hovered, ready to sweep and flood the ice. Now the Zamboni driver was waiting. He checked the clock.

Sam took one more shot at the net. He missed! The puck rang off the crossbar and whizzed into the spectator stands.

"YUCK!" snapped Sam, frustrated. He

stomped his skate. He banged his stick on the ice like a woodsman chopping wood. *"Arrgh!"*

Coach Howie looked up, turned around, and peered down the ice.

WHEEE!

He blew his whistle and pointed directly at Sam.

The Practice Rule

"Sam! Practice is over!" Coach Howie hollered. "Let's go! Pick up the pucks NOW!"

Sam banged his stick again. Ice chips flew.

"Hurry, Sam," Tom said in a quiet voice. His stomach began to knot. He didn't like it when his teammates got into trouble. He looked at Coach Howie, who shook his head and did not take his eyes off Sam.

Sam dragged his feet. He looked like he was moving in slow motion.

SWOOOOOOOOSH. SWOOOOOOOOSH. SWOOOOOOOOSH.

He straightened his shoulder pads. He twirled his stick. He waved at the spectators.

Finally Sam skated toward his fifteen teammates. They were filing off the ice and heading to the dressing room. As Sam passed through the gate, Coach Howie waved him over to the rubber mat. Coach Howie looked serious.

"Sam, cleanup time is a team activity. Did you hear the whistle?"

Sam leaned back and dropped his jaw.

"Remember the important hockey practice rule?" Coach Howie pointed to his ears.

Sam crossed his arms and looked up at the rafters. He nodded yes without smiling.

Tom and his buddies were at the back of the line. They could just barely hear what Coach Howie was saying.

7

Stuart whispered, "What's the rule? I don't remember."

"I only know *game* rules," said Tom.

"It's got something to do with cleanup and his ears. Maybe the rule is clean them out before hockey," suggested Mark.

"*Ughh*," Stuart groaned. "Yellow earwax is gross like brown toe jam. I think it's about listening."

"That's a no-brainer. Everyone knows you have to listen to your coach!" said Harty.

The boys moved closer to Sam. He was chewing on his popped-out mouthguard while he tapped his toe. He looked annoyed.

Coach Howie put his hand on Sam's shoulder and said, "Sam, you have good hockey skills. But on a team, *all* hockey players have to listen and have a positive attitude. It's called 'respect.'"

"But, but, but . . ." Sam argued, red-faced and rattled. He was thinking about all the goals he had scored for the team.

Coach Howie continued: "Tomorrow we have a big game, and it should be a good day for the *entire* team, including you. We need to work together on and off the ice. Okay?"

Sam sighed and nodded.

"Good," said Coach Howie, also nodding but looking skeptical. He hurried off to unlock the dressing room.

Sam strutted behind in a huff.

"I just saw smoke blasting out Sam's ears," said Mark, "barbecue-style."

"Barbecue?" chimed Harty and Jordan.

"Yeah. I could roast a marshmallow over his earlobe, he's so fired up!" said Mark.

Tom held up one hand to say, *stop*. "Hey, guys. Cool it. Sam's part of the team, and teammates work together. And like Stuart said . . . he's our goal getter."

What's Up, Sam?

The dressing room buzzed with laughter and hockey talk.

Tom and Harty peeled off their sock tape and added it to their giant tape balls. Stuart yanked off his elbow pads and checked for bruises. Mark pulled off his helmet, and his hair stood straight up like porcupine quills.

Sam *flumped* down on the bench next to Tom.

"Hey," said Tom.

Sam grunted.

Tom blushed.

"Settle down, Hawks! And listen up!" Coach Howie raised his arm and everyone sat up. The room became silent. "Hawks, I saw some great work out there today. I saw some strong skating and some powerful energy."

Sam took off his jersey while the team cheered, "Yay!"

Tom's "Yay!" was extra loud. He liked Coach Howie.

Coach Howie continued: "I saw some improvement in skills."

Sam gulped down the rest of his sports drink while the team cheered again.

Tom felt good about the day's practice. He had worked hard on his skating skills, especially the backward crossovers. He had concentrated on extending his leg and using his toe. *Yay!* Tom told himself. He was getting faster.

Tom clapped Harty on the back because he was getting faster, too. Together they could be two speedy skaters on the forward line.

Meanwhile, Sam looked bored with the team meeting. He got out his felt marker and marked his hockey stick with the number of goals he'd scored during the scrimmage.

Coach Howie rubbed his hands together and said, "Tomorrow's game is against the Grey Wolves."

"Their goalie is amazing," Jordan reminded the team. "He can stop pucks with one punch of his goalie blocker!"

"No worries," said Coach Howie, being positive. "We're ready for the Wolves! We'll have fun!"

The players looked at each other and chattered: "Yeah." *"Hmmm."* "Maybe." "Yes siree!" "Sort of." "I'm counting on Sam!"

"C'mon, Hawks!" said Coach Howie. "Where's our team spirit? Every player here has an important job on the ice . . . and on the players' bench. Let's *count* on teamwork! That's what works!"

"Yay!" everyone cheered — except Sam. He knew he was the best.

"Wow! I didn't know being on the players' bench was an important job," said Stuart. "That's when I have a drink of water. Sometimes I scratch an itchy spot."

"I already work hard at working hard," said Mark. "But I'll work harder!" He flexed his muscles. "I'm not afraid of the big bad Wolves!"

Chuckles circled the room.

"Now, have a great afternoon, Hawks! Get some rest. Eat healthy. See you tomorrow. I can't wait! We'll play great!" said Coach Howie, making everyone feel confident. He looked over at Sam and raised his eyebrows, as if to say, "Don't forget our talk about teamwork!"

Sam smiled when Coach Howie was looking but rolled his eyes and scowled when Coach Howie wasn't looking.

Tom didn't like Sam making faces behind

Coach Howie's back. *Does Sam make faces behind my back?* he wondered.

Tom bravely nudged him and asked, "What's up, Sam?"

Sam folded his arms and tilted his head.

"Huh? I didn't say anything." And he hadn't. It just seemed like he had.

"Oh," said Tom. It was weird. The way Sam moped and moved and stomped and hissed and huffed and pouted and smirked and glared and glowered and eyeball rolled was just like talking. And Tom could understand him perfectly.

What If?

The Hawks rolled their equipment bags out of the dressing room, down the hallway, and beneath the spectator stands. They headed for the arena entrance where their parents waited for them. Tom's dad was talking with Sam's mom. She gave Tom's dad a big grateful smile.

"Now it's time to work hard off the ice," announced Mark. "I'm going to down a whole meat-lover's pizza for lunch!" He snickered. "Pizza with pepperoni that's hot, hot, hot . . . will improve my hockey shot, shot, shot! And extra cheesy makes it easy!"

Everyone knew Mark played his best when he ate pizza. It was his good luck charm.

"No pizza for me!" said Stuart. "Last time I ate hot pizza I burned my mouth and couldn't wear my mouthguard."

"Oh boy," said Mark. "One time I got a big penalty for not wearing a mouthguard. I was taken right out of the game!"

Sam piped up, "What? You got taken out of the game? For that?" He frowned and made two thumbs-down.

"The ref called it," said Tom.

"It's a rule," said Jordan. "No mouthguard, no hockey — no arguing about it."

"There's no arguing with Coach Howie either," complained Sam. "He thinks I have something wrong with my ears. I think he has something wrong with his eyes. Doesn't he *see* how hard I try to win?" Sam made a sour face. "It's not fair. What's Coach Howie looking at? What *does* he see?"

Everyone shrugged their shoulders, but they knew what Coach Howie had seen.

Sam stuck out his tongue. "That's what I think."

Tom did not like to hear or *see* bad comments about his coach.

"Maybe Coach Howie needs glasses," suggested Stuart, trying to be positive. "I saw him squinting at you. And making his eyes bug out."

"*Hmmm* . . . Can you guys help me?" asked Sam. "I need to show Coach Howie how good I am."

Tom glanced at his friends. They all looked puzzled.

Mark spluttered out an offer: "What if we *assist* you? We'll pass you the puck every chance we get. Coach Howie will be impressed if you get a goal against the Grey Wolves!"

Sam's crabby face began to brighten. He gave Mark's idea two thumbs-up. "You guys promise to pass only to me?" He looked straight at them with hopeful eyes. "Come on, it's teamwork!" he coaxed. He nodded his head until everyone was nodding yes along with him, including Tom.

This type of teamwork made Tom feel uneasy. He knew he should pass to the player on the ice who is in the best position to receive the puck.

Sam reached out his right hand. "Let's shake on it with the Hawks' handshake!" he said, pumped.

Hesitantly, they all stuck their right hands out. They layered hand upon hand, like a salami sandwich, until there were six hands on top of each other.

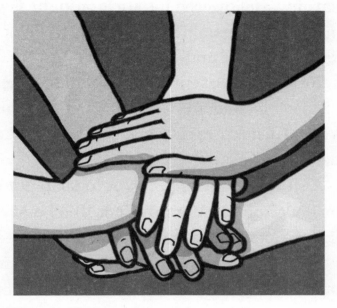

"Hawks!" they shouted.

"Cool," Sam said, looking smug. "I'm going to get a goal against the Wolves!"

"Hey, *stay* cool — real cool. That's what matters most," said Jordan, worried. "Their goalie is so good at stopping pucks his nickname is Stop Sign."

But Sam wasn't listening to Jordan's

warning. He lowered his stick onto the floor and ran off, using a wrist shot to flick a candy wrapper under a chair.

"He shoots. He scores!" Sam shouted back.

Stuart looked ill. "This is a risky plan! What if I mess up a pass? He'll be mad at me."

"All I wanted was . . . Sam to snap out of his lousy mood." Mark fretted. "Did I make a big mistake? This is not funny, guys."

"This is the worst. We gave him our Hawks' handshake promise," said Harty.

"Sam *made* us shake on it," blurted Mark. "He made us make a hand *Sam*wich! Now my nerves are fried like bacon."

Tom felt sick. He could barely breathe. "We're doomed. A promise is a promise when you shake on it. Coach Howie taught us to pass to everyone on the ice. Now this . . ."

"Stop Sign the goalie stops pucks," Jordan said one more time. "What if Sam can't get a goal? He might have a mega meltdown."

Everyone crossed their fingers and hoped for the best as they left the arena.

As Tom rolled his equipment bag down the ramp, his dad cheerfully said, "Hey. Sam's mom asked if Sam could come to our house tomorrow after the game. I said yes. You okay with that?"

Tom gasped and turned white. He looked like he'd been hit with a snowball.

Hockey Talk

Sunday.

Snow fell quietly around the city.

Inside Centennial Arena a crowd cheered and roared. The Glenlake Hawks Peewee One team was playing against the Bears. The score was 5–1 for the Bears.

Tom and his parents stopped to watch at the spectator glass. The Bears' winger had the puck. He went in for a shot on net. He scored!

"Na, na, na, na, na!" The scoring winger danced and wagged his stick at the Hawks' goalie.

The referee went into action. He blew his whistle and pointed at the net.

"Goal!" he announced. "Number 19." He pointed at the dancing Bear and made a T sign with both hands. "AND Number 19: two minutes for unsportsmanlike conduct."

"Yay!" "Wow!" "Huh? "Good." "Seriously?" "Fantastic!" The crowd went crazy as #19 slunk to the penalty box.

Tom was puzzled. "Hey, Dad. I thought the T signal was for when a coach wants a timeout to talk to his team."

"Well, Tom, that dude was rude. And the ref saw it. So he's getting a two-minute penalty." Dad nodded in agreement with the ref's call. He explained, "The T has two implications: It's the signal a coach uses for a time out with his team. But it's also the signal a ref makes for bad behaviour, and that is called unsportsmanlike conduct."

The Hawks and Bears faced off again, this time without #19.

"Go, Hawks, go!" Tom automatically cheered. And the Hawks kept going.

"Tom! We're in dressing room number four!" called Harty, racing by.

Tom bolted down the hallway, bubbling with excitement. "It's game day!"

They bombed through the doorway.

"Remember to drink water while on the players' bench . . ." Coach Howie was saying to Brett. He glanced over and smiled at the boys. "Hi, guys!"

"Hi, Coach!" chimed Tom and Harty.

Tom found a spot on the bench. He opened his hockey bag. *Ewww.* His hockey pads were still wet from practice.

"Yesterday was a doozy!" Tom said.

"Oh yeah!" Harty rubbed his calves. "My legs still hurt."

Stuart looked green. "Playing the Wolves today makes me woozy," he squeaked. "Everyone talks about the Wolves' great goalie. But I remember their good forwards. One guy always tries to sneak in the back door. I need to be on my toes to defend *our* net." Stuart bit his bottom lip. "I already have blisters on my feet."

"Stu, you are a super defenceman," said Tom with a thumbs-up.

Stuart brightened. "Yeah. I try my best."

As Tom tied his skates, Sam leaned over and whispered, "I have a secret."

"What is it?"

"I'm not allowing myself to smile until I get three goals today!" said Sam. "Good idea, eh? It's called 'having an incentive!'"

"Huh?" Tom didn't get it. "Three goals is a hat trick! That's a lot of goals."

"I'll do it," said Sam. "It's *my* goal. Just pass me the puck." He half-smiled by mistake.

Soon the team was dressed and ready. Coach Howie put on his lucky cap and gave a quick pep talk: "Let's show the Wolves our best! When you take a shot, put some mustard on it!" He gathered his notes and first aid kit. "Now let's play hockey!"

Sam looked fired up. "Of course I put mustard on it!"

Oh, man. Now Sam's going to turn into a

hot dog! thought Tom. *I smell trouble with our cooked-up plan.*

Warm-up

The fans took their seats in the stands. They clapped and waved at the two teams as the players launched onto the ice. Tom's mom held up a giant neon sign that read "HAWKS ROCK!" The O in the word *ROCK* was a smiley face.

The pre-game warm-up started. Coach Howie gave the scorekeeper a game sheet. He shook hands with the ref and the coach from the Grey Wolves.

Tom stretched and lunged as he glided forwards. His newly sharpened blades cut into the freshly flooded ice. He picked up his pace and cruised to the corner. He concentrated on the crossovers he'd worked on at practice the day before. Yes! He felt strong. He turned and skated backwards.

Grey Wolves zoomed by him. They took shots on their net to warm up their goalie.

BAM! BAM! BAM! went the puck, flinging off Stop Sign's blocker. It was no surprise.

Meanwhile, at the other end of the ice, the Hawks were warming up Jordan. He stopped puck after puck, until Sam took a shot.

SWOOSH!

The puck slid between Jordan's skates. Sam raised a fist for victory, but he did not smile.

"I'm wearing my lucky Band-Aids," Stuart announced as he skated alongside Tom. "They're yellow and green, our team colours!"

"Good job, Stu." Tom looked at the Grey

Wolves. They were huge. They were fast. The Hawks needed a case of lucky Band-Aids.

"I ate my lucky pizza for breakfast," said Mark, catching up. "But . . . the Wolves look like they ate raw buffalo guts for breakfast. I saw fangs on one guy."

All three boys gulped.

The Grey Wolves gathered together in a pack. They cheered loudly:

Wolves, Wolves,
Are the best.
Put those Hawks
To the test!
Yay, Wolves!

"Their cheer makes me want to howl back at them," said Mark. "Where's Sam? He can pass their test with flying pucks!"

"I'll pass their test," said Tom. "You will too!"

"Yeah, but Sam will huff and he'll puff and

he'll blow the puck down the ice and into their net." Mark calmed himself with a joke.

A group of Hawks stood by Sam.

"Sam, did you hear their cheer?"

"You show them, Sam!"

"Score, Sam, score!"

The pressure was on, and for the first time in a long time, Sam looked nervous.

After the warm-up, Coach Howie waved the team over. They huddled together and shouted, "HAWKS!"

Coach Howie clapped hard and said what he always said: "Now let's have fun!"

Jordan took one last swig of water and pulled down his scary goalie mask. *"Grrrr."* He was ready.

The first shift skated toward their starting positions. Sam was centre, Mark left wing, Harty right wing, with Tom and Stuart on defence.

"Rats," sighed Tom, slightly deflated. He usually played forward, and he didn't like playing defence. But with Sam on the forward line, there was no room for him.

It's okay, Tom told himself. *Me and Stu know what to do. We'll work together to defend our net.* He high-fived Stuart before they set up.

"Go Hawks!" yelled a fan.

Tom looked up. His mom waved her sign. "HAWKS ROCK!" She smiled just like the happy face in the word *ROCK*.

At centre ice, the referee blew his whistle and dropped the puck.

Game On!

Sam jabbed at the puck. He won the faceoff! The puck flew back to Tom. Tom sent it sailing right to Sam. Sam skated hard toward the net, stickhandling perfectly. Mark stayed with him on right wing, ready to assist.

The Wolves' defence moved in. Stop Sign, the goalie, kept his eyes on the puck and on Sam.

"Go, Hawks, go!" yelled the fans.

"Go, Sam, go!" yelled the players on the bench.

Sam took a shot and hit Stop Sign's blocker.

The puck rebounded. Mark and Harty hustled for it, but Sam swooped around. He caught the puck and fired another shot, right over Stop Sign's left shoulder.

DONK!

The puck landed in the net like a bird in a cage.

"Goal!"

"Yay!" the crowd cheered.

Tom's mom waved her poster up and down. "HAWKS ROCK!"

"Yay!" yelled the Hawks. "Yahoo!" They jumped for joy in the players' box. The skaters on the ice hugged Sam.

Sam happily tapped his stick on the ice. But he did not smile. He needed two more goals to smile.

"Sam *is* our man!" said Mark, nearly dancing. "Did you see that? I'm so glad Tom passed to him!"

The ref skated to the scorekeeper's window. "Goal for Hawks number 13. No assist," he announced.

Coach Howie made a shift change. Five new players went on the ice.

"Wow!" said Tom, sitting next to Sam on the players' bench. "We're less than one minute into this game and we've already scored."

Sam narrowed his eyes at Tom's comment. Tom quickly corrected himself: "Errr . . . I mean *you've* already scored your *first* goal today!"

Sam gloated. He liked getting a goal against the toughest goalie in the league. "Next time there won't be a rebound," he said. "I'll get the goal on my first shot."

"Show off," mumbled Harty as he moved into the lineup.

The ref dropped the puck for the next faceoff and the new players on the ice. The centres battled for the puck. This time the Wolves got control.

Sam shook his head. *"Ewww."*

The Wolves' #18 passed the puck to his left winger. She hit it against the boards. Now the Hawks' right defence stole the puck and passed it to their centre. It was a turnover.

For the next two minutes, the puck went end to end and side to side — back and forth and around the ice. It went from Hawks to

Hawks to Wolves to Hawks to Wolves to Wolves to Hawks . . . again and again. It seemed like forever.

Finally the Hawks took a shot.

Stop Sign bashed it away from the net.

"Go, Hawks, go!" yelled the Hawks' fans.

"Go, Wolves, go!" yelled the Wolves' fans.

Sam looked bored sitting on the players' bench. He picked at the old sock tape stuck on his knee. Meanwhile, the puck zipped from player to player. Tom's eyes following each move.

"Go, go, go! Almost there!" Tom could feel the rhythm of Hawks' #19 skating and receiving another pass. Tom held his breath. His eyes got big. "C'mon, Brett! You got it!"

Brett took a shot.

Stop Sign reached out and punched the puck with his glove. As Brett neared the net for the rebound, a Wolves' defenceman banged the puck to the opposite end of the rink.

Wheee!

The ref blew his whistle and raised his hand for an icing call.

Coach Howie rattled the metal latch on the gate to signal a line change. The tired and winded Hawks skated off the ice.

Tom smiled and gave them high-fives as they reached for their water bottles. "Great job, guys!"

Sam rolled his eyes. He tapped his toe and stared at Coach Howie. Sam scrunched his forehead as if to say, "You'd better keep me on the ice full-time if you want to win!"

Coach Howie didn't do that.

The third shift took their positions. Forty-five seconds later, the Wolves did a quick tic-tac-toe passing play. They scored!

"Yay, Wolves!" yelled their fans.

Wolves, Wolves are the best!

Put those Hawks to the test!

It was now 1–1.

Sam dropped his shoulders and flung his head back. He blew out a big mad breath as he watched the numbers on the scoreboard change. He threw out a look that said, "What happened?"

The skaters left the ice with their heads down. They avoided Sam's steely stare.

Tom, Harty, Stuart and Mark high-fived their teammates. "Good try, guys!" they told that shift.

Sam did not high-five. Instead, he held his head high and strutted out to centre ice.

The first shift was back.

Down and Out

PLOP!

The ref dropped the puck at centre ice. This time the Wolves won the faceoff.

Sam lunged and stretched. He scooped up the puck in one quick swish. He charged forwards, chased by the Wolves.

Their defence closed in.

"I'm here!" called Harty. He positioned himself perfectly.

"Over here!" called Mark.

Both Hawks' wingers were ready for a pass. Sam didn't pass. Instead he took a weak flip shot. The puck skipped right into the Wolves' defensive zone. The right defenceman nabbed the puck and barrelled ahead. He passed it to the tricky left winger.

Sam threw his arms in the air and stomped his skate.

Stuart battled for the puck in the corner. Tom protected the front of their net. Finally they got a break. Tom grabbed the puck and controlled it with his blade.

"Go, Tom!" yelled his Grandpa.

Tom skated forwards, his heart pounding, and then he remembered the Hawks' handshake promise. He passed to Sam.

The Wolves stopped the puck midway.

Mark got the puck back. He passed to Sam.

The Wolves stole the puck just as Sam was about to touch it.

Harty got the puck back. He passed to Sam.

Sam took a shot and scored!

"Yay!" cheered the Hawks and the fans.

"I got the assist," Harty said quietly.

Sam pointed to himself. His face said: I got the goal.

At the end of the first period, the scoreboard read 2–1 for the Hawks.

During the second period, the Wolves' fans hollered their cheer louder. Sam stomped his skates harder. But the score stayed the same.

— ● —

It was now halfway through the third period. The Wolves' coach called for a time out. "We need a plan," she said.

The Wolves shared their observations.

"The Hawks keep passing to their centre!" exclaimed the right winger. "Then he hogs the puck."

"Puck hogs always make mistakes," huffed a defenceman.

"Let's *wolf* him down!" added their centre.

"*Awoooo!*" they howled, hungry for a goal.

The first shifts headed back on the ice. They skated to their positions.

The puck dropped.

The rush was on.

Now all the Wolves were watching Sam like a hawk!

They hovered around Sam and waited for the puck to come his way. They pounced on the puck before he could get it.

Sam was getting frustrated. He was like a Hawk being caged.

Harty, Mark, Tom and Stuart were tired of feeding the puck to Sam. It was not working. It was not the right thing to do. Their nerves were on edge and it was trouble.

"What's happening out there?" Coach Howie shook his head, confused.

Finally Sam got the puck. He shot it.

Stop Sign stopped it with his stick. Sam caught the rebound. Stop Sign went up and down, side to side, in and out of the net until . . . Sam raised his stick to take a slapshot . . .

SHWOOOP!

He swept the air and missed the puck altogether. That's when the Wolves' #3 snuck in and cleared the puck out of Sam's way. His stick was like a windshield wiper, wiping away a giant black bug.

BLAM! Sam bashed his stick on the ice. He was so busy being mad he forgot to chase the puck. He forgot to help his teammates. He forgot how to play hockey.

"Yay! Wolves!" screamed their fans. "Go, Zippy, go!" they shouted to their #3.

"*Ughhrrrr!*" Sam fumed as he watched Zippy bolt to the blue line and score with a one-timer.

Thunk went Tom's heart.

The puck had flown right between Tom and Stuart . . . like a bullet.

It was now tied 2–2.

Coach Howie called for a shift change. "Good try," he told Tom and Stuart as they entered the players' box. "But start passing to different players on the ice. You need to mix it up to keep the Wolves on their toes."

"Okay," agreed Tom, Harty, Stuart and Mark. They all had long faces as they reached for their water bottles.

"We've kept our promise to Sam," Tom whispered. "We said we'd pass to him. We did. We're done."

Harty, Stuart and Mark nodded.

"Sorry, the deal's off," Tom told Sam quietly and bravely.

Sam paid no attention. He threw his stick against the bench and carried on, rattled and fuming. "*Grrrrzzch!*"

"Cool down, Sam," said Coach Howie

Sam crossed his arms and pouted. He kicked his skates and scoffed. "*Blech!*"

Stuart blinked back tears.

Harty frowned. "I want to play on a different shift," he said. "I don't want to be on the ice with *him*. I feel rammed by Sam."

"No kidding," stated Mark. "I'm done with Sam the Ham. He's a puck hog and dishes out baloney!"

Tom turned away. He stood at the boards with his back to Sam. "Let's cheer for the players on the ice! They need our help!" said Tom, pointing to the action. The players were fighting hard for the puck. "C'mon, Hawks! YOU ROCK!"

Tom's words filled the skaters with powerful energy.

Sam stewed. He steamed. His face was red and sweaty.

The rest of the team watched the game at the boards. They chanted "Hawks! Hawks! Hawks!"

"Stay strong!" encouraged Tom.

The Wolves' #4 made a smooth turn behind the net. She slammed the puck over Jordan's stick. Goal! It was now 3–2 for the Wolves.

Sam moved to the gate for his next shift. He sneered at the players leaving the ice. They hung their heads. But Coach Howie and Tom picked them up with a pat on the back.

"Good try, guys."

Sam rolled his eyes and grunted. That's when Coach Howie made the letter T with his hands.

"Sam! Timeout! You are not going back on the ice."

Sam screwed up his face as if to say, "What? Why? Really? Huh?"

Whump!

He hurled himself onto the bench.

Everyone was stunned, but they all seemed to agree that Sam deserved the T for unsportsmanlike conduct.

Coach Howie stayed cool. He said, "This shift I want Tom to play centre, and Brett, you go in on defence."

Tom loved playing centre. But out of the corner of his eye he could see Sam making a mean face targeted right at him.

Ouch! thought Tom. *Sam makes me feel bad about my hockey.*

"*Pfft!*" scoffed Sam.

"Enough." Tom's heart was aching. He didn't have one more positive, cheer-up-you're-great boost to give Sam. He edged over and looked Sam right in the eyes. "Stop bringing us down."

Tom stood tall and skated off to take his position on the ice. He did not look back.

Now *Tom* was playing centre, his favourite position. He was determined to play his best.

Game Over

BOOM! BOOM! BOOM!

Spectators banged drums.

A cowbell clanged.

The fans wearing yellow and green hollered, "Hawks!"

Harty's sisters chanted their cheer:

> *One, two, three, four.*
> *Try your best,*
> *Score one more.*
> *Five, six, seven, eight.*
> *You are Hawks.*
> *You are great!*

PLUNK!

The ref dropped the puck.

The Wolves' centre won the faceoff.

Tom grabbed the puck and zipped ahead in high gear. He passed to Mark. Mark passed to Harty. They all skated hard.

"Go, Hawks!" shouted the crowd, giving the players extra zest.

Harty passed to Tom. Tom unleashed his wicked slapshot. The puck soared into the net. GOAL!

"Yahoo!"

"Yay!"

"Way to go, Tom!"

The boys high-fived on the ice.

The whole team high-fived on the bench — except Sam. His hands were on his hips.

Tom's mom waved her sign. "HAWKS ROCK!"

Tom glowed.

The game was now tied at 3–3.

Coach Howie signalled the skaters to stay on the ice for the final minute.

The Wolves' coach put their fastest and strongest players out.

Tom hustled back to centre ice thinking, *These guys might be foxy Grey Wolves, but when the Hawks work together, we're GOLDEN!*

As the clock counted down 5, 4, 3 . . . Stuart sent a puck flying through the air like a flying saucer. It whizzed by the Wolves' forwards. It blazed past their left defender. It was heading right for Stop Sign's dreaded blocker. He was ready to stop that puck.

"Oh no!" Tom's eyes bulged.

SWOOOOOOSH!

Stop Sign missed.

WHEEE!

The ref blew his whistle and pointed at the net. "Goal," he called out, "for the Hawks!"

BUZZZZZ!

The final buzzer sounded. The Hawks won!

"Yay, Stu!" hollered Tom. He skated over for another high-five.

"Yaaaaaay!" the fans went bonkers.

"Yaaaaaaaaaay!" the team went crazy. Except for Sam — he went woozy. He was sitting in the players' box feeling mighty shocked. The Hawks had won without him.

"*Whoo-hoo!*" Stuart's feet did a happy

dance until the Band-Aid popped off his big blister.

The team bolted onto the ice. They jumped and squealed. They huddled around Stuart and their tired goalie, Jordan.

"Yahoo!" they whooped and hugged.

Coach Howie looked happy.

Everyone was happy . . . except for Sam. He didn't understand why Coach Howie had kept him off the ice. "I didn't do anything. I didn't say anything," he repeated over and over. "It's not fair."

The team was too busy to notice moody Sam. They were on the ice together, shaking hands with the Wolves and saying things like "Thanks for the game." "Good game." "See you next time." "Nice zip, Zippy!"

When the handshakes were finished, the Hawks threw their hockey gloves into the air.

"Yay, Hawks!" they cheered once more, this time circling around Coach Howie.

"Good job!" Coach Howie's smile was as wide as a banana.

Cool It

Mark cranked up his music in the dressing room. He belted out:

We are the champions of the rink,
And we make our hockey gear stink!
We are the best team.
We make our fans scream.
YAY!

Coach Howie clapped and smiled.

"Congratulations, Hawks! We had a lot of fun today! The Wolves put us to the test!"

The Hawks patted each other on the back.

"Awesome goal!" Tom told Stuart one more time.

"Thanks, buddy!" said Stuart. "You assisted me!"

Tom felt proud.

Sam huffed, and stuffed his hockey equipment into his bag. He yanked the zipper. He didn't act like a champ even though he'd scored two goals.

— ● —

The Hawks hurried out of the dressing room and scrambled toward the snack shop and greeting area.

Tom's parents were waiting by the popcorn machine. "Tom! Sam! Over here!" called Tom's mom.

"Oh no!" Tom winced with dread. "Not today!" He'd forgotten Sam was going to his house after the game. It was bad enough being with Sam on the bench and ice.

Tom looked over his shoulder and saw Coach Howie talking to Sam by the trophy case.

POP-POP-POPPITY-POPPITY-POP! went the popcorn machine.

"What's up?" asked Stuart scrunching his face. "What's Coach Howie telling Sam?"

"All I heard was 'Stop your popping!' Sometimes Coach Howie says weird stuff," said Tom.

"All I see is hands talking," said Mark. "Coach Howie looks like he's directing traffic in a storm."

Grrrrr! Jordan's stomach rumbled. "Right now my stomach is talking. It's telling me to have lunch!"

Mark opened a bag of pickle chips and passed it around.

"Are we playing shinny at the outdoor rink after lunch?" asked Harty.

"Well . . ." Tom felt like he was *in* a pickle. How could he tell his friends about Sam? He looked away and confessed, "Sam's coming to my house right now."

"Why?" grumbled Mark.

"I've had enough of him. I'm sick of him rolling his eyeballs at me. He makes me feel . . ." Stuart did a plummeting thumbs-down.

"He makes me want to roll my eyes in spirals back at him!" Mark slurped his juice box. "This is the last straw! Sam can make his nest with the robins, 'cause he's *robbin'* the Hawks of our *Hawky* fun!"

"No kidding!" said Jordan.

"I can't help it! My dad told his mom that he could hang out with us! So he's coming over to play shinny," said Tom, flustered. "I'm stuck with him!"

"Errr . . . ah . . . I'm cleaning my bedroom," said Jordan.

"Sorry. I've got homework," said Harty.

Stuart faked a sneeze.

"I'll think of something else to do," quipped Mark with a mischievous glint in his eye. "Like write a poem."

Tom gave them his extra disappointed look. "This is not good," he sighed. *Nobody wants to be with Sam . . . including me.*

——●——

The road outside the arena was snow covered and busy. Tom and Sam sat in the back seat of the truck staring out their windows. Tom's parents took turns asking them questions, trying to stir up a conversation.

"Is this Sam's first time to our house?"

"Are you boys hungry?"

"Which NHL team is the best?"

"Who likes having a snow day?"

"You guys okay back there?"

Tom's mom turned around and gave them one of her looks. It said, "Something's fishy."

Tom didn't smile. He didn't argue. He didn't laugh. He didn't look happy. He wanted to play shinny with his *real* friends, and it was not happening.

Sam nudged Tom. "Why are you so mad at me? Everybody seems to be mad at me. What did I do," he said, in a quiet voice, "except try to win the game?"

HONK! HONK! HONNNNNNNNNK!

An angry driver leaned on the car horn and shook his fist as he drove by.

"That driver makes me want to shake my fist too, but I won't do that. I'll just keep my cool," Tom's dad said. "It's cool to stay cool."

"That guy should learn my secret *trick*," said Tom's mom. "When things don't go my way, I start counting to one hundred. By the time I get to about twenty-two, I'm all cooled down — like a cucumber."

They turned the corner and the truck tires

got stuck in a giant rut. They began to spin, and Tom's parents started counting, "One, two, three, four . . ."

The HAWKS ROCK! sign sat on the floor of the truck. None of their faces looked happy like the smiley face on the sign.

Body Language

Tom's mom set the kitchen table for two. "Dad and I need to shovel the sidewalk. But you guys seem like hungry bears, so sit down and eat your lunch." She carried over two bowls of green vegetable soup. "There's extra milk in the fridge and cheese buns in the toaster. Enjoy!" she said.

"Thanks," said Tom.

"Why are you mad at me?" Sam asked. "Come on."

Tom shrugged his shoulders. He didn't quite know how to tell him. Then Tom had a flashback to the game. Sam had been a ham, a hot dog, a sourpuss, a cranky pants, mean and a rude dude — all without saying a word.

"What did Coach Howie tell you?" asked Tom.

"He said, 'From your head to your toes, your body *shows* what you are thinking. It's called "body language" . . . and it communicates a message.'" Sam humphed. "I'm supposed to get some good vibes going . . . whatever *that* means."

Tom raised his eyebrows and leaned in closer to Sam, wanting to hear more.

"Coach Howie told me winning isn't everything. Having fun and having good sportsmanship makes *real* winners." Sam swallowed hard. "He won't let me go on the ice when I'm *showing* a bad attitude." Sam made the T sign. "That's what I'll get — a big timeout!"

"*Hmmm* . . ." Tom scratched his head,

trying to compute what he'd just heard.

"I thought winning *was* everything." Sam blew on his hot soup. After a few moments, he said, "I just made a wish to win . . . more friends at hockey."

"You could win more friends if you really wanted to," said Tom.

"How?"

Tom saw his chance. He sat up straight, took a deep breath, and tried his best to explain: "Well . . . I like being your hockey friend when you're in a good mood, but not when you are in a bad mood. That's when you upset the whole team and forget about teamwork. A bad attitude spoils everything. It stinks!" Tom gulped. He could feel his nerves tingle.

Sam folded his arms. "No way! I never forget about the team! I even have a Hawk pillowcase to dream about the team! And

I wear yellow and green underwear for team spirit!" He rolled his eyes and began to pout. His lips were pressed together so tightly bubbles foamed in the corners of his mouth.

Oh man. This is exactly what I'm talking about, thought Tom. He wanted to give up. His brain was spinning. He wished Sam could see himself just then, getting into a nasty mood all over again.

POP!

Cheese buns popped out of the toaster. As Tom reached for them, he saw his reflection on the shiny silver toaster. It was like a mirror.

"Bingo! That's it!"

"Huh?" said Sam.

Tom pointed to Sam's reflection.

Sam took an extra-long look at the poisonous pouty face he was making.

"*Ewww*," he choked. "*Errr . . . Ummm . . .*
Do I really look like this?"

"Yup," said Tom, trying to be helpful.
"Sometimes worse."

"Worse? Yikes!" Sam's cheeks turned as
red as a chili pepper. "I guess I wouldn't
want to play hockey with *that guy* either. He
looks cranky and mean."

"Sometimes you do this when the team
does something you don't like . . ." Tom

lifted his lip, bugged his eyes and flared his nostrils. "And when you are bored with the team, you do this . . ." Tom fake-yawned and tapped one foot. He ended his imitations with a stomp, grunt, raised arms and rolling eyeballs.

"What?!" Sam panicked. "You see all that?"

"Yup!"

"What about the team?"

"Yup. The whole team notices — the spectators and the Zamboni driver, too." Tom spread his arms wide as if to say, "The whole world is watching you."

"*Ewww.* I stink like a rotten egg!" Sam plugged his nose and sank into his chair.

Eggs-actly, thought Tom.

After a few seconds Sam added, "I heard someone call me a bad apple."

"Oh no. Not a bad apple." Tom braced himself, waiting for Sam to get mad.

But he didn't. Sam wiped his eyes as he got up from the table.

"Sometimes I get so bent out of shape my stomach hurts."

"Well . . . that was *then!*" said Tom. "This is *now!*"

Sam paced back and forth. Suddenly he knew what to do. Sam made a big toothy clown smile and checked out his reflection on the shiny refrigerator door. "What do you think, Tom?"

"Wowzers!" Tom gasped. "You look like you just won the Stanley Cup!"

"Yay!" Sam put two thumbs up and broke into a happy dance. "No more being a rotten egg who spoils everything! I'll *think* before I make a big stink!"

Tom gave Sam a high-five. "Now you're talking!"

Sam did one last spin, his eyes catching

his cheerful reflection. That's when he realized something: "I can use body language to say good stuff, too!"

Tom choked on a piece of broccoli. Green bits sprayed out his mouth.

Sam passed Tom a napkin to wipe his face. With two fingers, he made the peace sign for Tom. "I don't want Coach Howie to give me another timeout! I can't let that happen again! I like being on the ice with the team because I love hockey!"

It was amazing. Mega miraculous! The toaster had warmed Sam up. The refrigerator had fed him refreshing moves and good vibes. Tom peace-signed him back.

"And . . . I'm going to use your mom's count-to-one-hundred, cool-your-jets trick when I'm getting frustrated," said Sam, "to chill out — like a cucumber."

"Wow! You got it!" Tom shook Sam's hand,

thinking, *Sam is like a super genius, he's caught on so fast.*

Tom felt great. Now he could breathe easily. His old happy Hawk self was back!

"Let's eat quick and get to the rink! It's shinny time!"

They downed their lunch.

No Stink
at the Rink

Crunch! Crunch! Crunch!

Tom and Sam trudged along the snow-packed path with their helmets, gloves, sticks and skates.

"I call this path the Hockey Highway!" Tom said. "'Cause it leads right to the rink!"

They picked up the pace. They checked out the ice to see who was there.

"Look at all the little kids." Sam frowned. "Where are Stuart, Mark, Harty and Jordan?"

"Not coming."

"What?" Sam's shoulders slumped. "Because of me?" Sam didn't wait for the answer. "Oh man. I really messed up." He bashed his stick on the snowbank.

Stuart's younger sister, Kaitlyn, skated over.

"Hi, Tom," she said. "You guys can join our shinny game. But . . ." She cringed. "We're still learning."

"*Hmmm.* I don't think . . ." Sam was about to make an unfriendly sour face, but stopped.

Tom shot Sam a look.

Sam could tell what Tom was thinking. It was written all over his face. *Remember? Be nice.*

"What am I doing?" Sam mumbled. He shook his head and plugged his nose as a signal to himself: *don't make a big stink.* He turned his lips into a smile and replied, "Okey-dokey!"

"Awesome!" squealed Kaitlyn. She popped up two thumbs. "You can show us what to do."

"Great!" said Tom. But he thought, *What if something doesn't go Sam's way? We'll have to go home.*

"Let's go!" said Sam.

"Let go!" said Tom as they joined the game.

The orange plastic puck zigzagged across the ice — back and forth. It landed on top of the net. It hit a tree. Henry sat on it twice.

Sam stomped his foot and groaned, "*Ugh!*"

Kaitlyn and Charlie stomped their feet, following Sam's lead. "*Ugh!*" he echoed.

"Don't scowl at me," Henry said sadly. "I know some of my hockey is *UGH*-lee!"

Kaitlyn and Charlie gulped.

"No way!" Sam coughed out. "I didn't mean to *ugh*. I wasn't thinking," he confessed. "Our coach always says, 'We're here to have fun!'" He slapped Henry a high-five. "A puck landing dead on top of the net is the coolest hockey shot I've ever seen."

Henry giggled. "That shot *was* pretty funny. I *almost* went in the net!"

"I saw it," said Charlie.

"Me too," said Kaitlyn.

They high-fived all around.

"Phew," sighed Tom. "Sick!" He loved the way Sam turned around a bad situation. "Nice save." He gave Sam a wink and tapped the puck back into play.

Sam cheered on Kaitlyn and her friends with encouraging words: "Good try!" "Next time!" "Yay!" "Yahoo!" "Hooray!" He topped it off with thumbs-up and enthusiastic clapping.

"*Whoo-hoo!*" Kaitlyn whooped happily.

Tom flashed Sam the A-OK sign.

The game played on. Soon more kids and neighbours joined in. Sam took a turn in goal. The puck flew over his stick and into the net — five times.

"Playing goalie is hard," he said, discouraged. His face was turning purple, purplier and then purpliest.

Tom watched, eyes bulging. Would Sam smash his stick on the crossbar, have a meltdown, and throw his gloves off? "Hang in there, buddy!" offered Tom.

"Give me a sec," said Sam. He took a big swig of water and gave himself a pep talk.

"Be a cucumber!" He plugged his nose and clenched his teeth.

The other players cheered Sam on.

"Keep trying!"

"We don't keep score here!"

Sam took another deep breath. Then he stopped the next shot on goal. "Yes!" He pumped his goalie blocker in the air.

Tom and Sam were having so much fun they forgot about the unfun part of the day.

When it was time to go home, Kaitlyn said, "Hey, Tom. We like your new friend."

"He's a good sport!" exclaimed Henry.

"He's a good nose plugger," teased Charlie.

Tom and Sam grinned.

"How cool is that?" they said at the same time.

"I don't think Kaitlyn recognized me from the team!" said Sam. "Weird, eh?"

"Weird," Tom agreed.

On the way back to Tom's house, the two friends batted a tennis ball back and forth with their hockey sticks.

Right then they both felt like winners.

But what about tomorrow? worried Tom.

Happy Hawks Rock!

It was four o'clock on Monday. Wild music blared in the dressing room at Centennial Arena while the Hawks suited up for practice.

A few players spread out their gear, making no room for Sam.

Sam paid no attention. Today was a new day. He was wearing a team hat and his yellow and green long underwear. "Hey, guys!" he shouted over the noise. "How ya doing?"

Mark answered, "I didn't like missing

shinny at the rink. It made me grumpy. So I wrote this poem:

> *Down with the frown.*
> *Out with the pout.*
> *Off with the scoff.*
> *In with the grin.*
> *Just think . . .*
> *I'm not a grump,*
> *When I jump,*
> *At the rink!*

Tom cracked up watching Mark jump for joy on one foot. "You look like a player with ants in his hockey pants!"

"Sweet!" said Mark as he leapt across the room.

Tom felt jumpy, too. He was excited and nervous. He looked at Sam and wondered, *What's next?*

Sam hummed a cheerful tune while taping his hockey socks. When he was finished, he

B. Nobody argued. He explained the drills. Nobody interrupted.

"Okay, Hawks," said Coach Howie. "Let's get the show on the ice!" Everyone grabbed a puck and began to stickhandle it around the ice while weaving around the pylons.

Stuart took off like a rocket. He blasted by the first two pylons then caught an edge. He spun like a propeller and crash-landed near the boards. "*Oooof!*"

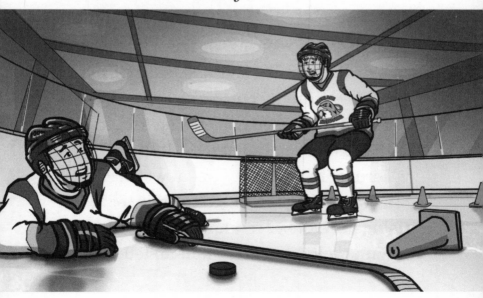

Sam stopped. "You okay?" he asked.

"Nothing hurts." said Stuart struggling to get up.

Sam reached out his hand to help.

"I'm good," Stuart said, red-faced and embarrassed.

"One time I tripped during the pylon drill," whispered Sam. "I *piled on* the pylon, and the pylon got stuck on top of my helmet. I looked like I had an orange cone head!"

"Really?" Stuart relaxed. "Hey, thanks."

"Let's keep skating. We're almost at the fire drill." Sam led the way, skating perfect crossovers on the corner.

Jordan crouched in net. The skaters took a shot as they paraded by.

Jordan moved left. He moved right. He was practising Stop Sign's goalie technique, using his blocker to knock the puck.

Sam took a powerful well-aimed shot.

BAM!

Jordan got it.

"Nice save!" exclaimed Sam.

Jordan nodded happily. He squinted his eyes. *Was that really Sam?* he wondered.

Sam circled back and skillfully shot a puck into the net.

"Great goal!" said Jordan.

There were fifteen minutes left. Coach Howie blew his whistle. He waved the team over to the bench. "It's scrimmage time. Group A against Group B," he said. "What's the number one thing we should be working on?"

"Passing the puck to everyone," suggested Sam.

"Right on!" stated Coach Howie.

"Wow! Sam the Ham, the rude dude is gone," whispered Mark. "I am beginning to like him."

"Me too," admitted Stuart, Harty and Jordan.

Coach Howie gave Sam a thumbs-up. "You're looking good today, Sam!"

"I'm working hard on teamwork by giving it my BEST SHOT!" Sam promised the team. "Because I have had a major breakaway!" He put a smile on his face the size of a boomerang.

"I think you mean a 'major breakthrough,'" said Coach Howie. He clapped hard. "That's a T for *Terrific*! Right?"

Sam looked around. The team was tapping their sticks on the ice as a way of saying, "Yay, Sam!"

Tom wished he had a shiny refrigerator door with him so Sam could see his happy hockey body language in the reflection.

"Now let's have fun!" said Coach Howie. He zipped up his jacket and pulled a new puck out of the pocket.

"Wow! Coach Howie rocks!" said Sam for the first time. He met Tom's eyes. "Hawks rock!"

The players set up.

"Game on!" Tom beamed, totally pumped. "Hold on to your hockey helmets! This is going to be the best scrimmage ever!"